The
Princess Present

MEG CABOT

The
Princess Present

A Princess Diaries Book

◼ HARPERCOLLINS*PUBLISHERS*

The Princess Present

Printed in the United States of America. For information address HarperCollins Children's Books, a division of HarperCollins Publishers, 1350 Avenue of the Americas, New York, NY 10019.

www.harperteen.com

Library of Congress Cataloging-in-Publication Data
Cabot, Meg.
  The princess present : a princess diaries book / Meg Cabot.—
1st ed.
    p.   cm.—(The princess diaries)
  Summary: In a series of diary entries, Princess Mia describes celebrating Christmas with her friends in Genovia.
  ISBN 0-06-075433-8
  [1. Princesses—Fiction. 2. Christmas—Fiction. 3. Diaries—Fiction. 4. Humorous stories.] I. Title. II. Series.
PZ7.C11165Pue 2004
[Fic]—dc22   2004008597
                                                        CIP
                                                         AC

Typography by Alison Donalty
1 3 5 7 9 10 8 6 4 2
❖
First Edition

ACKNOWLEDGMENTS

Many thanks to Beth Ader, Julie Beckham,
Jennifer Brown, Barb Cabot,
Sarah Davies, Michele Jaffe,
Laura Langlie, Abigail McAden,
and especially
Benjamin Egnatz.

"It has been hard to be a princess today . . ."
she said. "It has been harder than usual."

A LITTLE PRINCESS
Frances Hodgson Burnett

Tuesday, December 22, Noon,
Royal Genovian Bedchamber

OH, MY GOD, THEY'RE COMING!!!! HERE!!!! THEY'RE COMING HERE!!! THEY'LL BE HERE TOMORROW!!!!

Why am I the only one who CARES???? Grandmère just looked up from her lemon juice and warm water and went, "Prepare the blue and gold wing, please," to Antoine, the majordomo.

AND THAT WAS IT.

She is so tied up with planning her Christmas Eve Ball (royalty from all over the world will be descending on Genovia for it), that she can't think of anything else. Not that anybody else in the family cares about it. Dad even asked why we couldn't just have a quiet family Christmas for a change.

Grandmère looked at him with daggers in her eyes and then said, as she sorted through all the RSVPs she'd gotten in the mail, "Well, if Prince Nikolaos of Greece thinks we're going to put up his polo pony while he's here, he is sadly mistaken."

My dad just sighed and went back to reading *The Wall Street Journal*.

I am telling you, there is something WRONG with my family.

"Hello? That's *it*?" I cried. "The future Prince Michael Moscovitz Renaldo is arriving tomorrow for his first visit ever to the country over which he will one day help me rule, and all you can say is *'Prepare the blue and gold wing, Antoine'*?"

That got my dad to look out from behind his newspaper.

"You two are engaged?" There was this total crease in the middle of his forehead. Funny how I've never noticed it before. If I stuck a penny in there, I bet a gum ball would fall out of his mouth. "When did this happen?"

Sadly, I was forced to admit that Michael had not, as yet, proposed.

But it's sure to happen eventually, as a love like the one Michael and I share can never be denied— no matter what the studios who make all those movies allegedly based on my life might think.

"Oh," my dad said. And lost all interest. The crease completely disappeared. In fact, his whole head disappeared back behind the newspaper.

"Fresh cut flowers will be placed in all the rooms in the blue and gold wing, Amelia," Grandmère said, as she banged on the end of her soft-boiled egg with a silver spoon. "What more do you want? A gala in the young man's honor? As if we don't have enough to worry about with the Christmas Ball. Why must you obsess so over such inconsequential things?"

Inconsequential? INCONSEQUENTIAL? Michael and Lilly's first ever visit to Genovia is INCONSEQUENTIAL? I mean, sure, they're only coming for a week . . . a mere seven days . . . only one hundred and sixty-eight hours. . . .

But I'm trying to stay positive, like Dr. Phil says to.

"A week isn't very long to enjoy all the incredible sights this country has to offer."

That's what Philomena, my dad's latest girlfriend, had to offer to the breakfast convo. Like this wasn't a completely transparent attempt to get in good with my dad. You know, on account of her appreciating his native land so much. Like he was going to throw down his paper and be all, "Philomena, light of my heart, be mine forever!" because she said you couldn't see everything there is to see in his principality in seven days.

Whatever.

Not that I don't wholly support a woman's right to use her god-given assets to get a prince to propose to her, or to make a career out of strutting down a runway in a thong with a pair of wings attached to the straps of her bra.

I just, you know, hope she's socking some of it away in a decent 401(k) or some Roth IRAs.

Grandmère ignored Philomena. This is her custom where my dad's girlfriends are concerned.

"You must be sure to remind Antoine to secure a tuxedo for your young man," is all Grandmère said. "I don't want him turning up at the ball in dungarees. And tell Lilly I expect her to have removed all of those horrid friendship bracelets she wears. Straggly pieces of dirt-collecting yarn is what I call them. I won't have the Contessa Trevanni thinking my granddaughter's best friend is a bag lady."

The whole time she was talking, Rommel, Grandmère's hairless toy poodle, was totally looking on, so hoping she might drop a crumb or two of the toast she was smearing with soft-boiled egg guts. Because Rommel is on this diet where all he's allowed to eat is specially formulated dog food. This is on account of the royal vet recently diagnosing him with irritable bowel syndrome. Apparently, the IBS is caused by the antidepressants Rommel is taking to combat his OCD, which manifests itself in his licking all of his fur off.

"And the parents of your little friends don't mind them spending Christmas away from home?" Philomena asked, all sweetly.

"No," I explained to her, speaking slowly because she's Danish. And a model. "The Moscovitzes don't celebrate Christmas. They're Jewish."

"And they are coming on the Royal Genovian jet?" Philomena asked, her perfectly plucked eyebrows raised. Because she'd had to fly commercial to get to the palace—first class, but still—on account of the jet having been sent to pick up Michael and Lilly.

"Certain people," my dad said from behind the paper, "refused to spend the holidays in Genovia—on the grounds that she'd miss her baby brother's first Christmas—unless certain demands were met."

Philomena looked confused, apparently not realizing my dad was talking about me and the temper tantrum that had finally forced him to send the jet for Lilly and Michael.

"But that's terrible," Philomena said in her Danish accent. "Who would rather stay in America for the holidays than come to this beautiful place?"

Really, I don't know how I'm supposed to endure the anti-Americanism that is rampant in this part of the world. Sometimes it just makes my blood boil.

But whatever.

THEY'RE COMING!!!! They'll be here in twenty-four hours!!!! I have to get to work if I'm going to have everything ready for them in time.

TO DO LIST:

1. Make sure Michael gets the Prince Guillaume Royal Memorial Bedchamber, the one with the panoramic view of the Genovian Bay—and not just because its balcony is right next to mine and we can sneak out at night and climb over the railings and watch the moon rise in each other's arms. Michael! My love! It's been three whole days since last we met!

2. Have Antoine put the good guest soaps in their rooms, and not the cruddy soap made from Genovian olive oil with the royal crest printed on it, which never foams up.

3. Make sure the palace kitchen has Heinz ketchup, because that's the only kind Lilly likes.

4. MAKE SURE SATELLITE TV IS HOOKED UP IN ALL BEDROOMS!

5. Find out what is up with my hair.

6. Make sure there are plenty of copies of smart magazines like *The New Yorker* and

Time lying around, not just *Us Weekly* and *CosmoGIRL*. Don't want Michael assuming all I think about is celebrities and my appearance!

7. Crest Whitestrips. Get them. Use them.
8. Cuticles. I have totally let them go. And now they're all gross and bloody looking. Just the kind of look a girl wants for her hands when she hasn't seen her boyfriend in three days.
9. TOENAILS!!!! CUT THEM!!!! I'm starting to look like one of those rhesus monkeys.
10. Double-check Christmas shopping list:

Dad—Subscription to Golf Digest. *Done.*

Grandmère—Padded satin hangers, per usual. She herself said a princess can never have too many. Done.

Philomena—What DOES the modern princess

get for her dad's latest skank? I'm thinking
Pussy Pucker Pots vegan lip balm, so at least
Dad won't be ingesting harmful animal
by-products every time he sticks his tongue
in her mouth. Done.

Mom—Yoga pants. Not that she does yoga.
But she loves anything with elastic waistbands
at this point in her battle to lose her leftover
pregnancy weight. Done.

Mr. G—Bose headphones so we don't have to
listen to his AC/DC. Done.

Rocky—Baby Mozart video, since research
suggests that a relationship exists between expo-
sure to Mozart's music and increases in spatial
reasoning abilities and intelligence, and I don't
want Rocky to suffer the way I am when HE gets
to Geometry. Done.

Fat Louie—Catnip in a sock. He's not picky. Done.

Lars—Renew his subscription to Guns & Ammo. *Done.*

Tina—Book on how to write a romance novel and get it published. Done.

Ling Su—Paintbrushes . . . NOT ones made out of animal fur. Done.

Shameeka—All the episodes of The O.C. *I secretly taped for her since she isn't allowed to watch that show. Done.*

Boris—Copy of the Queer Eye for the Straight Guy *guide to dressing better. Done.*

Lilly—Copy of If I'm So Wonderful, Why Am I Still Single? Ten Strategies That Will Change Your Love Life Forever. *It is very hard to figure out what to get for Lilly and Michael, because they celebrate Hannukah and that amounts to EIGHT nights of one present*

*each as opposed to ONE day when you're
LUCKY if you get eight presents. And even
though Lilly says most of her presents are things
like underwear and socks, I can't help feeling
like Jewish kids get a way better deal out of their
holiday than we do of ours. Although Lilly says
it is murder trying to think up eight gifts for her
dad, because how many ties and/or magazine
subscriptions can you give one person?*

Pavlov and Rommel—Rawhide chew toys. Done.

*Michael—This is the really hard one. I have
to get Michael something totally good for
Christmas, because the Hannukah gift I gave
him was such a bust. I guess I should have
known, because Dance Dance Revolution Party
for PlayStation 2 was something I wanted. I just
assumed he'd want it, too. Well, okay, I knew he
wouldn't really want it, but I thought once he
saw how FUN it was, he'd want it, too. But I
can tell he never uses it unless I come over*

because the floor pad is always exactly the way I folded it the last time.

So now I totally have to come through with something GREAT for Christmas to make up for my Hannukah GAFFE. So I'm getting him an original single-sided 27 x 41-inch movie poster from the 1977 George Lucas classic *Star Wars,* in near mint condition, according to the seller on eBay who I'm trying to buy it from. It will look very nice in Michael's dorm room. The bidding is at $23.72, with two days left to go. I put in $50 as my top bid. Nobody better bid more than me or I'll be forced to kill myself, on account of how I had to sell my precious Fiesta Giles *Buffy the Vampire Slayer* action figure just to get enough money to be able to afford Michael's gift (which blows because except for Military Xander, which I was missing, I had the complete set). Plus I only got $28 for Giles in his sombrero, so it looks like I'm going to have to dip into my savings.

But that's okay. Michael is sooooooo worth it.

From the Desk of
Princess Amelia Renaldo

Dear Antoine,

I know you are busy preparing the blue and gold wing for the Moscovitzes, who will be arriving tomorrow. I just thought I would let you know a few things you might want to put in each of their rooms to make them feel at home:

Michael Moscovitz:

- Telescope (that really big one from the royal planetarium will do)
- PowerMac G5 with 23-inch Cinema Display and AirPort Extreme Base Station
- CD player and the Flaming Lips' *Yoshimi Battles the Pink Robots*

Lilly Moscovitz:
- Segway Human Transporter
- *DSM-IV-TR Diagnostic and Statistical Manual of Mental Disorders*
- CD player and Lash's *The Beautiful and the Damned*

Also, mini-fridges in each room filled with Yoo-Hoo and chocolate-covered pretzels for late-night snacking would be very much appreciated.

HRH Mia Thermopolis

I perfectly understand my dad objecting to buying a
Segway Human Transporter for Lilly. But he didn't
have to be so crabby about it. They have totally fixed
them so they don't have that problem where they
flop over anymore.

Also, I think one would be quite handy for, say,
reviewing the Royal Genovian troops. You would
think my dad would appreciate my efforts to get the
palace to move into the twenty-first century. But I
guess not.

I don't know why Grandmère threw such a fit
over my Christmas list, either. I think all of the
things I asked for were perfectly reasonable:

Mia Thermopolis's Christmas Wish List:

1. World peace
2. Save the endangered sea turtle
3. iPod and PowerBook with $100 gift card to

iTunes online Music Store

4. Universal indoor smoking ban

5. TiVo

6. End to world hunger

7. Military Xander *BTVS* action figure

8. Segway Human Transporter

9. Eliminate fossil fuel emissions contributing to global warming

10. Ab Roller so I can look like Britney Spears

What's wrong with all that, I'd like to know? You can get the Ab Roller right off the Home Shopping Network. And they sell Segways on Amazon.com!

Whatever. Like I don't have bigger stuff to worry about. They'll be here in twelve hours!!!!! I went and checked their rooms, and Antoine didn't get them a single thing I asked him to. Instead of the *DSM*, he put a copy of *The History of Genovia* in Lilly's room. And instead of a telescope, he put BINOCULARS in Michael's room. (I took them. The last thing I need is for Michael to discover that the German tourists down on the Genovian beach like to sunbathe topless. Like I need that kind of competition!)

And there was no Yoo-Hoo in the mini-fridges. Just Orangina! Like orange soda goes with chocolate-covered pretzels! EW! You would think Antoine had never drank SunnyD then eaten an Oreo in his life. A combo as disgusting as that can scar the taste buds for life.

That's not the worst of it, though. The worst is that tonight at dinner, Tante Simone was fully asking me if I was going to dance with Prince William at the ball, and when I said no, Grandmère went BERSERK. In front of Philomena and Dad and Prince René and Sebastiano (who are here for the holidays) and the footmen and EVERYBODY!!!

Then Tante Jean Marie got into the act, and started saying all this stuff about how there are a lot of fish in the sea and I shouldn't limit myself at such a young age to one person, especially someone who isn't even of royal blood himself. I don't know where those three get off—Grandmère and her sisters, I mean. They have their OWN château, Miragnac, right down the road. Why don't they ever stay THERE? I mean, I know Grandmère feels like she has to hang around the palace to act as hostess since there is none, but—

Oh, my God, how am I supposed to concentrate with that hideous noise coming from outside? I understand that people are excited that it's nearly Christmas, but they ought to show some respect for others by not CATERWAULING underneath other people's royal bedroom balconies. . . .

Wednesday, December 23, 1 a.m.,
Royal Genovian Bedchamber

It wasn't drunk tourists making all that noise under my balcony after all. It was the sweetest little black-and-white cat! Why can't people take better care of their pets? I swear, she must have been starving. When I left, she was still chowing on the two pounds of leftover lobster Thermidor I stole from the royal kitchen for her. But she'd already managed to put away most of the caviar.

Anyway, let's see, where was I?

Oh, yes. My totally embarrassing family. I swear, if any of them says anything about how I should dance with Prince William while Michael is here, I am fully going *Chasing Liberty* on them.

Ten hours until they get here! I have GOT to get some sleep, or I'll have puffy eyes AND a giant zit tomorrow. I found one on my chin just now. I globbed a pile of toothpaste on it so hopefully it will be gone by morning.

Wednesday, December 23, Noon, Royal Palace Toilette

They're here!!!!!!!!!

Oh, my God, it was SO WEIRD to see Lilly and Michael with, like, palm trees and the ocean in the background. They got out of the limo all blinking from the bright Mediterranean sunlight and stuff, and I rushed up and was all, "Welcome to Genovia!" and they looked around at the Royal Guard standing at arms by the palace doors and all the tourists pressed up against the gates they'd just driven through, snapping photos and going, "There she is! The Princess of Genovia! Mort, get a picture!"

And Lilly went, "You LIVE here? It's bigger than the freaking Met," which is, you know, an understandable reaction, I guess. I mean, she's only seen photos of the palace before. It IS sort of over-whelming when you find out there are thirty-two bedrooms, a ballroom, two pools (outdoor and indoor), a home theater, and a bowling alley (Grandpère routinely scored in the high two hundreds).

And when Franco, the footman, came up and tried to take Lilly's Emily Rocks! DJ bag from her, she snatched it back and was like, "Dude, that's MINE."

But then I gently explained that Franco was a royal footman and that he gets paid to help carry palace guests' stuff.

So then Lilly got all excited and gave Franco her wheelie bag and her CD player and her peacoat and her Royal Genovian jet sleeping mask and her Doc Martens, which she'd been wearing around her neck, since they wouldn't fit into her bag and she'd worn her moon boots for comfort on the transatlantic flight.

All Michael did was grab and kiss me. Which you can bet plenty of tourists got snaps of. I heard them all going, "Quick! Did you get that? We can make a fortune selling it to the *Enquirer*!" as their digital cameras clicked away.

So now Lilly and Michael are "freshening up" because that's what Grandmère makes every single overnight guest who arrives at the palace do as soon as they get here. I showed them to their rooms myself (well, Franco followed, along with Antoine, who was all worried about the Yoo-Hoo slipup) and I'm glad to say my fears were for nothing. They both seemed perfectly happy with the rooms they'd been assigned . . . especially Michael, when I pointed out the thing about our balconies being right next door to each other.

After they're "freshened," Antoine's supposed to take them on a tour of the palace while I do a quick photo op with Dad and Grandmère and the Fabergé Advent calendar in the Hall of Mirrors.

But after that, we can hang all day.

Well, until I have to go light the Christmas tree in the Genovian town square.

But then we can do whatever we want!!!

Um, until dinner, anyway. Some of the guests for tomorrow night's ball have already started arriving, and I promised Dad and Grandmère I'd help entertain the younger royals.

But then after that, we'll be free for fun for sure!!!!

Disaster.

First of all, I don't know what's wrong with Lilly. I mean, I KNOW that the palace is filled with riches that, if sold, could feed hundreds of thousands of starving people. The Fabergé Advent calendar alone—being an exact replica of the Genovian palace, only in Fabergé's version, each shuttered window can be opened to reveal a perfectly cut jewel, one for every day of Advent—is insured for $17 million.

But hello. The Fabergé Advent calendar is not MINE. The da Vinci sketches in the Galerie aren't mine, either. I do not own the Rembrandts in the Great Hall or the Rodin in the royal garden or even the Monet hanging over the bathtub in my own royal bathing chamber.

Yet.

And until I do own them, I can't sell them and donate the money to Oxfam or Human Rights Watch, the way Lilly seems to think I should.

And what was all that about the gross materialism of Christmas while we were at the tree lighting? Hello. All I did was plug in the tree in the middle of the town square while everybody stood around clapping. Is it my fault that after the ceremony they all went back to the baccarat tables? Tourism is responsible for a very significant portion of Genovia's economy, and a big draw for the tourists is gambling.

And Genovia uses a lot of that money to help the poor, as I pointed out to Lilly on our way back to the palace. Hello, we don't even make our citizens pay TAXES.

But Lilly just went on making rude remarks, until even Michael, who is the most even-tempered of men, finally turned around and was like, "Lilly. Shut *up*."

Of course she didn't listen to him. And I knew it was only going to get worse when, after we all went to change for dinner, Lilly showed up in the Crystal Pavilion where we'd gathered for premeal Kir royales wearing her WWJJD (What Would Joan Jett Do?) T-shirt and a pair of low-rise jeans that I happen to know for a fact her mom expressly forbade her to wear in public. I practically had to throw myself on her to keep Grandmère from spying it and having a cocktail hour embolism.

"Lilly," I whispered, "what are you doing in that? I told you, dinner here is a very formal affair."

"Oh, what," Lilly said, looking disgusted. "You want me to dress like that hoser over there?" She pointed at Camilla Parker-Bowles. "Yeah, because pink taffeta so suits my personality."

"No," I said. "But you could at least show some respect for my dad, who went to all the trouble of sending the jet for you and is putting you up for a week. I mean, you think Michael is happy wearing that suit?"

We both looked over at Michael, who was tugging at his shirt collar while having a very in-depth conversation about cyclotron frequency with Prince Andrew. Uncomfortable in his suit as Michael clearly was, he still looked totally hot.

"See?" I glared at Lilly. "Your brother knows enough not to insult his host. Why don't you?"

Lilly rolled her eyes.

"Fine," she said. "I'll change. But you gotta show

me how to get back to my room. This place is so huge, I took a wrong turn and ended up in some bowling alley. . . ."

I looked around and saw Franco passing by with a tray of canapés. I signaled to him, and he came right over, and said he'd be only too happy to show Miss Moscovitz back to her room. So the two of them left . . . for an extraordinarily long time, actually.

But by the time Lilly got back (just before Antoine came out and announced that dinner was served), she'd changed into a Betsey Johnson number that at least didn't have any writing on it, so I thought everything would be all right.

Yeah. Right.

I don't know whose idea it was to seat Lilly between my cousins René and Pierre, the thirteen-year-old Comte de Brissac. All I know is that midway through the soup course, René threw down his napkin, got up, and stormed off, muttering French swear words and saying something about how it was the fascists who drove his family from their ancestral Italian palace, not inbreeding, as Lilly had apparently suggested.

He didn't come back until dessert, and even then, he took a seat at the far end of the table, vacated by one elderly duke with an apparent incontinence problem, and sat scowling into his blancmange.

Pierre, however, didn't seem to have a problem with Lilly. In fact, he stared at her throughout the seven-course meal in a manner reminiscent of the way Seth stared at Summer in the early episodes of *The O.C.*

But attacking my family members was apparently not enough for Lilly. She had to start in on Philomena next . . .

. . . which really, if you think about it, is totally beneath her. I mean, for someone of Lilly's abilities—and she scored a 210 on an online IQ test we took together earlier that year; I only got a 120 (although on the EMOTIONAL IQ test, I got a 120, and she only got a 90)—goading Philomena is like shooting rubber bands at rats on the subway tracks.

"So, Philo," Lilly began conversationally. "You meet a lot of princes in your line of work?"

Philomena smiled and went, "Oh, no, not so many."

"So when you finally do meet one, you really have to hang on to him," Lilly said in a this-is-just-between-us-girls tone.

"Oh, well," Philomena said with a laugh, glancing at my dad to see if he was listening—he wasn't. He was talking to King Juan Carlos of Spain about golf. "Yes, of course."

"Because," Lilly went on in the same conspiratorial manner, "seeing as how you make your living on your looks and never bothered to pursue any kind of higher education, as soon as your boobs start to sag your modeling agency will kick you out on your butt and you won't have two euros to rub together, will you? So you better marry a prince— or a rock star—pronto or it's buh-bye to those four-hundred-dollar highlights, right?"

"Lilly," I said, starting to get up. "Can I have a word with you in the salon?"

"No need," Lilly said with a dazzling smile. "Oh, look. The cheese course."

Fortunately Philomena lacked a firm enough grasp of the English language—or was simply too dumb—to have understood what Lilly was saying to her. She just smiled and looked confused, her usual expression.

Pierre, however, looked totally impressed. I even heard him murmur, over his St. André triple cream, "Mademoiselle, you intoxicate me."

To which Lilly replied, "You have Roquefort on your cravat, kid."

As if all that wasn't bad enough, after dinner, when the adults went into the salon for cigars and port and gossip and I was left to entertain the younger royals with Fanta, some spoons, and a deck of cards, Lilly looked around, yawned, and said, "Jet lag. Going to bed. See you tomorrow," and vanished!

Michael and I were forced to play spoons for TWO HOURS with Pierre and a bunch of other under-twenty-one royals . . . who, by the way, weren't very impressed with the game. Simon, Lord Mulberry, a distant Windsor cousin, kept asking why we couldn't play strip poker instead.

You know, you would have thought that all of us royals would get along much better, considering each and every one of us (well, except Michael) has the weight of a throne resting upon our teenaged shoulders, and several of us know what it's like to have movies made about our lives . . . movies that aren't exactly strictly FACTUAL, if you know what I mean, and take a certain number of LIBERTIES with the truth.

I don't know how Michael managed to stay awake, having just come from another time zone, and all. I know MY eyes were drooping, and I'd had three days to get used to Genovian time already. I barely even managed to kiss him good night before stumbling into my room and into bed.

As if all of that isn't bad enough, someone topped my $50 bid on Michael's *Star Wars* poster! With only twelve hours left on the bidding, I put in a high bid of $75. With expedited shipping to get it here by Christmas, I am only just barely going to be able—

Oh, my God. What is that? Someone is at my balcony door!

Oooooh. Not someone. *Michael.*

Suddenly I don't feel so sleepy anymore. . . .

Thursday, December 24, 1 a.m.,
Royal Genovian Bedchamber

Oh, my God, I can't *believe* what just happened! Michael and I were having a lovely time making out on my balcony under the stars, with the scent of bougainvillea filling our nostrils and the glow of the Christmas tree downtown just enough for us to see by, when suddenly we were interrupted by the most unearthly wail. . . . I swear, I thought the ghost of Prince Guillaume, in whose memorial bedchamber Michael is supposed to be sleeping, had come back to get all in my face about kissing a nonroyal—

Only it turned out, it wasn't the ghost of Prince Guillaume. It was that little black-and-white cat again!

Only this time, she'd brought a friend! Not just one, it turned out. But five. Five little starving friends!

Michael was against feeding them. He said that would just make them come around more often. But what was I supposed to do, let them starve before my eyes?

Michael said they didn't look too starved to him, and pointed out—after I'd dragged him down to the garden to see how cute they were for himself—that they all seemed well within normal weight and that one was even wearing a collar.

But I know from having seen so many episodes of *Miracle Pets* that just because a cat is wearing a collar doesn't mean it isn't starving or a long, long way from home. For instance, one couple lost their cat when it climbed into a neighbor's moving van. They didn't see it again for three months, when they received a call from a fur trapper in Alaska, three thousand miles away, who said he'd found their cat in a tree outside his cabin and did they want it back?

So we snuck into the royal kitchen and scraped up some leftover crown roast and filet of sole to feed the poor starving things.

And you could tell they were really grateful because the hum of their mutual purr as they chowed down was almost as loud as the beat of waves down on the beach below.

After all of that, of course, Michael could fight his jet lag no longer, not even for kissing.

But that's all right, because there's always tomorrow night!!!! The best Christmas present I could ever ask for would be another night of kissing Michael under the Genovian night sky.

One weird thing, though: When Michael and I were coming back upstairs from feeding the cats, I thought I saw Franco, the footman, leaving the blue and gold wing, looking kind of . . . flushed.

I wonder what he could have been doing there?

Oh, well, maybe Lilly woke up in the middle of the night and needed an egg cream or something. I'll ask her in the morning.

I can't believe Michael is sleeping in the room RIGHT NEXT DOOR to mine. Only a single wall—and a bathroom with a Jacuzzi tub and all of the plumbing to operate it—separates us! Good night, my cherished preserver! Sleep well!

Oh, my gosh, I hope that if I snore he doesn't hear me through the wall.

Thursday, December 24, 5 p.m.,
Royal Genovian Bedchamber

A MUCH better day so far than yesterday. Actually, one of the best days I've ever spent in Genovia!

For one thing, I WON THE *STAR WARS* POSTER!!!! Yes!!! I was the highest bidder!!! I have already contacted the seller, and he agreed to air express it so it arrives in time for Christmas tomorrow.

YES!!!!!!!!!!!! She shoots, she scores.

As if that wasn't good enough, Lilly was actually in a good mood today. She was laughing and joking from breakfast on. It was like she'd turned, overnight, into a different person. She didn't go out of her way to antagonize Grandmère or even Prince René (who nevertheless gave her a wide berth, announcing that he was going skeet shooting with Mrs. Parker-Bowles and the Prince of Wales, and not returning to the palace until teatime). She didn't say a word about the seven pounds of kippers at the breakfast buffet, and even seemed to have fun dipping slivers of buttered toast into her first ever soft-boiled egg.

Then, the truly miraculous thing occurred: Grandmère—who was bustling around with a walkie-talkie, barking orders at Antoine, as more and more royals (Princess Mathilde of Belgium's glider almost landed on the conservatory) poured in from all over Europe and beyond—commanded us to leave the palace. Grandmère said she was tired of having so many children underfoot. And so she'd ordered that the royal yacht take us on a cruise up and down the Genovian coast for the rest of the day!

And, okay, we had to take the other teenaged—and younger—royals with us.

But still! A day at sea, instead of hanging around, shaking the gifts under the twenty-foot-tall Christmas tree in the Great Hall and concluding that none of them was big enough to be a Segway, and being forced to stand around at boring holiday events like the hideous rite of the olive branch, in which the youngest member of the family (namely, me) has to take an olive oil–soaked branch and poke it around in the fireplace while muttering stuff about wishing the family health and happiness for the coming year, while everybody else gets to swig grappa, aka hard liquor made from the leftover grape stuff after pressing.

Um, hello. I'll take the day at sea.

You can see why I fought so hard to stay in New York for the holidays. My mom and Mr. G's only holiday tradition includes decorating a tree with cutout portraits of famous people who died during the previous year, and then ordering in Peking duck from Number One Noodle Son and eating it while watching *A Christmas Story* for the nine millionth time. Heaven.

Anyway, we all went to change into our maritime clothes (jeans and a sweater for Michael; khakis and a windbreaker for me; overalls and a shirt that said TOUGHTITTIES for Lilly—but it was okay because the overall bib hid it; chinos, a navy blue blazer, and a red and gold tie for Pierre, Princes William and Harry, and the other male royals; Lilly Pulitzer everything for the Princesses of York and the females on the Grimaldi side of the family, who, by the way, are still pretending we aren't related).

I wanted to bring Princess Aiko of Japan along SO badly (she is officially the cutest royal I have ever seen), but her mom wouldn't let me even when I explained that, having a very young sibling myself back home for whom I am often sole caretaker—Rocky's father being, you know, a man, and my mother being an anarchist—I am probably the most responsible royal on the planet to leave a small child with.

But Princess Masako totally didn't go for it. Bummer.

Once we got down to the pier where the boat was waiting, I passed out nondrowsiness formula Dramamine to anyone who wanted some (Michael and Lilly took me up on the offer, but none of the royals did. Some of the Windsors, who shall remain nameless—okay, Lord Mulberry—even sneered at me. Gosh, I'm sorry. Just because you've spent every holiday of your life on a yacht or a set of skis, don't scoff at those of us who haven't. I'd like to see you figure out how to get from Fourteenth and Ninth Avenue all the way to Seventy-seventh and Lex with a single swipe of your Metrocard. Ha! Bet you don't feel so cocky now, do you, Your High and Mightynesses?).

Captain Marco had us out of the Genovian harbor—past all of the smaller yachts belonging to the German tourists, as well as the colossally huge cruise ship that had pulled in so its passengers could spend Christmas Eve in Genovia—and at sea in no time. It was really beautiful once we were skimming along the deep blue water, the wind in our hair and the sun on our faces.

It was too cold to swim, of course, but it got quite toasty, sitting in the sun, swilling down Orangina and nibbling shrimp cocktail. So toasty, in fact, that some of the boys had to remove their blazers. I kept a close eye on Michael, and was totally rewarded for my efforts by catching an eyeful of naked chest when he finally pulled his sweater off. Because part of his T-shirt came off with it, before he had a chance to tug it down again.

In all, a *very* lovely day.

There was a BIT of weirdness when I went over to Lilly's deck chair to ask her if she wanted any caprese salad and I saw Lord Mulberry sitting beside her. Their heads—her dark one and his reddish one, were kind of close together.

Which is odd because Lilly is virulently opposed to the British monarchy. The idea of taxation to support an unelected head of state offends her, and she says she eagerly awaits the downfall of England's aristocracy (she says Genovia is okay because we don't tax our citizens . . . which is why so many people want to move here).

Still, somehow it didn't look to me as if Lilly was sharing this opinion with Lord Mulberry, who happens to be twentieth in line to the British throne. Especially since, when I walked up to them, he was laughing at something she'd said as if it were the most hilarious joke he had ever heard.

When he saw me, though, he clammed up and went, "There's a man I've got to see about a dog." Then he moved to the front of the boat. Even though I happen to know the only people up there were some of my Grimaldi cousins, who are allergic to dogs. Or at least that's what they say to Grandmère whenever she asks them to dog-sit for Rommel.

But when I asked Lilly what that had been all about, she said she and Lord Mulberry had just been discussing the weather.

When I walked away, though, the Comte de Brissac sprang out from behind a lifeboat and informed me in a low voice that Lord Mulberry had been "pestering Mademoiselle Moscovitz" all day long.

. . . and then, as if that were not enough, Franco the footman had come by so often to ask Lilly if she needed anything, such as foot rubs or the *Herald Tribune*, that he (Pierre) believed Franco was "taking liberties" and would have liked to have seen "that hireling flogged for his overfamiliarity with the young lady."

To which the only sane reply was, "You are one weird little dude, Pierre."

But the Comte totally took it as a compliment. He bowed and went, "I feel it my duty to watch out for the fairer sex at all times."

So then I went back to Lilly's deck chair and asked her if Lord Mulberry was bothering her and if Franco had been overfamiliar.

Lilly tilted her sunglasses so she could see me properly and went, "Huh?"

So I explained what the Comte had said he'd seen, and Lilly snorted, lowered her sunglasses again, and said, "That little French weasel. Franco's just doing his job. And Lord Mulberry was only putting sunscreen on the backs of my calves where I couldn't reach." I noticed that she'd rolled up the legs of her overalls. "He was being quite helpful."

"Oh," I said. "Well . . . I guess that's all right then."

But when I went to report this to Pierre, he only laughed cynically and said, "Have you ever had a problem reaching the backs of your calves by yourself, Princesse? I myself have not."

Hmmm. I think maybe Lilly is starting to like the lifestyle of the rich and royal a little *too* much.

Still. It was a nice day. No one got pushed into

the water, and one of the Princesses of York even caught a fish!

Now we all have to get changed for the ball. I already checked Lilly's wardrobe, and she has a totally nice black satin and tulle number with a pink ribbon to wear (thank God Dr. Moscovitz insisted on a trip to Neiman Marcus before putting Lilly on the plane). Grandmère ought to have no complaints.

And I happened to catch a glimpse of Michael just now through his balcony doors (I was NOT spying. I had to go out on the balcony to see whether or not it was chilly enough for the satin stole that came with my dress) in his tux and all I can say is . . . move over, Orlando Bloom.

I don't care what Grandmère says. I did NOT ruin her ball. I DIDN'T.

Lilly did.

Well, it was MOSTLY Lilly, anyway. I'll admit she had a bit of help.

Everything was going fine until they made me dance with Prince William. How was I supposed to keep an eye on Lilly when I was so nervous that my boyfriend might, at any moment, grab the heir to the throne of England in a fit of jealous rage and break his nose? Not that Michael even appeared to NOTICE that I was dancing with someone else, so absorbed was he in his conversation with Prince Carl Philip of Sweden on the role of enzymes and gene regulatory elements in biotechnology and genetic engineering.

Still, a girl can dream.

Anyway, in my disappointment that Michael was not in the least bit jealous over my dancing with the most eligible bachelor in the world, I forgot to watch what Lilly was doing. . . .

And that's when Pierre came running into the middle of the ballroom—his tails flying behind him like a cape—slid to a halt in his patent leather dancing slippers, and screamed, "Stop them! Somebody stop them!"

Of course Grandmère immediately assumed someone was trying to steal the Fabergé Advent calendar. She tore herself from the arms of the guy she'd been dancing with—who turned out to have been Prince Hashem of Jordan—and charged after the Comte, shrieking, "Not the Fabergé! Anything but the Fabergé!"

But when we all dashed after him, we found the Comte headed toward the bowling alley, not the Hall of Mirrors.

And it was in that bowling alley that we were met by the most horrifying sight I personally have ever witnessed: Lilly, with about seven or eight of the young royals—whose identities I dare not record even in my own diary in case the paparazzi someday get their hands on it—engaged in a game of what can only be described as . . .

Strip bowling.

As if seeing Lilly making a strike in her Hello Kitty underwear wasn't bad enough, we were even more flabbergasted to see an enraged Franco throw down the tray of canapés he'd been carrying and challenge one extremely famous young royal of the male persuasion (who'd been keeping score in nothing but a pair of tighty-whities) to a duel over Lilly's honor!

The effect of this sight on the ball attendees was electrifying, to say the least. Prince René grinned and strode forward as if he were about to join the game—until my dad put a restraining hand on his shoulder, that is. The Contessa Trevanni gasped and threw her hands over her granddaughter's eyes, to shield her from the shocking sight. Prince Charles's ears turned as red as a pair of traffic stoplights. Prince William immediately started snapping photos with his cell phone camera, apparently with the intent of blackmailing a certain relative of his at a later date. The young Comte pointed at Lilly and cried in anguished tones, "I'd have treated you like a queen . . . but I won't be your bitch!"

The tighty-whitied royal told Franco that he had no intention of fighting anybody, at which point Franco stripped off one of his white gloves and slapped him across the face with it . . . in direct violation of Royal Genovian Footman guidelines.

At which point Prince René immediately began going around taking bets on the outcome of the fight, as a second later, a certain Windsor's fist connected with Franco's gut. The poor little Comte had to be physically held back—who knew Princess Anne was so strong?—to be kept from throwing himself into the fight as well.

I think it might have been all right in the end if the two fighters hadn't tumbled through the doors to the bowling alley and then into the Hall of Mirrors . . .

"NOT THE FABERGÉ," screamed Grandmère.

But it was too late. A second later, the brawling men rolled into the table holding the Fabergé Advent calendar, sending it crashing to the floor.

At which point Grandmère fainted dead away.

Thank God Michael and Prince Philip were standing near enough to catch her.

"We need to get her some air," Michael said in a commanding tone. Really, he is so good in a crisis. It's kind of thrilling to watch. "Out of the way!"

Everyone's bodyguards scurried to make room while Michael and Prince Philip—with the help of my dad—carried Grandmère toward the nearest set of French doors, which happened to lead out into the garden. . . .

. . . the same garden in which I'd discovered that poor little black-and-white cat.

Only instead of only bringing by four or five of her friends, tonight she'd brought about seven or eight . . .

. . . dozen.

The entire garden was filled with crying cats. White cats. Gray cats. Calico cats. Fat cats. Thin cats. Cats draped in trees. Cats lounging on the side of the fountain. Cats sitting on top of the stone wall. More cats than I had ever seen in one place in my whole life.

And all of them meowing for more lobster Thermidor.

Everyone stood staring at the cats in stunned silence until one of them—the little black-and-white cat I'd befriended in the first place—came sauntering up and started rubbing her head against my legs, through the silky satin of my evening gown.

At which point Grandmère raised her head, opened her eyes, took in the scene with a disbelieving look on her face, then glanced toward me and screamed, "MIA!!!!!!!!!!!!"

Well. At least for once she remembered to call me by my real name for a change.

Too tired to write. More later.

Friday, December 25, 8 a.m., Royal Genovian Bedchamber

It's Christmas. But I don't see anything too merry about it.

Last night was a total debacle. Between the naked royals—not to mention Lilly—the fight between a certain Windsor and Franco (sadly for René, a winner could not immediately be determined, as the fracas was broken up too quickly by the Royal Genovian Guard), the Advent calendar (apparently, it can be salvaged . . . but not in time for use for next year), and the cats, Grandmère's Christmas Eve Ball will probably go down in history as Genovia's most disastrous party of all time.

I can't even sleep anymore because the sound of all the car doors being slammed by indignant royals getting into their Rolls-Royces and being driven away keeps waking me up. Most of them—according to Jeanette, one of the maids, who just came in with a tray of hot chocolate for me—are claiming to have allergies to cat dander.

But you so know a big part of why they're leaving is that they want to keep their kids away from Lilly's bad influence. Even the prince and princess of Japan, and THEIR kid is only four or whatever.

Though to be fair, some of those teen royals . . . let's just say I highly doubt this is the first time most of them—particularly those Grimaldis—have ever participated in a game of strip bowling.

Oh, well. At least now my dad will have the quiet Christmas he wanted in the first place.

I guess I should get dressed and go see what's going on downstairs. I know it can't be good.

Well, the gift giving has begun.

Dad really seemed to like his subscription to *Golf Digest*. And even Grandmère couldn't help looking pleased at her padded satin hangers. She kept a pretty stiff upper lip all through breakfast and church, not mentioning a word about what happened last night, even when Lilly showed up at the table in the sweats she wears as pajamas. At least she'd put on the Genovian Palace terry cloth robe Antoine had hung in all the guest rooms.

It looked kind of funny with her moon boots though.

I expected Lilly to apologize—not to me but to Grandmère, at least. Instead, she just reached for some toast and started buttering it. I guess she's still upset about my dad firing Franco for striking a royal.

But, really, it's not like my dad had any choice. I mean, Prince Charles might very well have pressed charges. He didn't, thank God. But he COULD have. He settled instead for dragging his sons and Lord Mulberry off to Ibiza for the weekend, in the hopes that a run-in with Paris Hilton would negate Lilly's influence.

Lilly, for her part, argued that Franco had been rendered temporarily insane by his passion for her, and that it was wrong to deprive a man of his livelihood for momentarily letting his id get the best of him.

But Franco, with surprising dignity, told her that he didn't need her to fight his battles for him. Then he turned his footman livery over to Antoine, and strode from the palace forever.

Lilly wept, and said she and Franco had a relationship that was stronger than mere friendship or love. But since she'd said the exact same thing about a busboy just last year—not to mention Lord Mulberry just the night before—I can't say I was too impressed.

I noticed Michael didn't look impressed, either. He studiously ignored his sister all through breakfast, so I did the same. Although it was kind of hard, since it was just Michael, Lilly, Dad, Tantes Simone and Jean Marie, and Grandmère and me at the table. Philomena was still in bed, claiming to have a migraine (which might actually have been the smartest thing she's ever done); Prince René had run off with the Contessa Trevanni's granddaughter, much to the Contessa's delight; and Sebastiano had crept away in the early hours with Prince Albert, leaving behind a breakfast table set for a hundred, and enough bacon to clog the arteries of the entire country of Bulgaria.

After church, Grandmère announced that the gift exchange was to proceed, so we're sitting here opening packages. Back home in New York, we just open all the presents at the same time and are done in ten minutes. Here in Genovia, Grandmère likes to go around in a circle, having each person open one present, then show it to everyone, and thank the giver personally. It takes HOURS.

Here is what I have gotten so far:

• Dolce & Gabbana pink cashmere leg warmers (from Philomena)

- Ballerina music box from Tante Simone (who persists in thinking I am still nine years old)
- Hand-crocheted muffler from Tante Jean Marie. Because you know it gets so cold in Genovia (median year-round temperature 70 degrees)
- Copy of *America's Queen: The Life of Jacqueline Kennedy Onassis* from Sebastiano, who considers Jackie O the epitome of beaut (beauty) after Prin Di (Princess Diana)
- An electric razor from Paolo (very funny. Not)
- The Princess Mia Madame Alexander doll from Mamaw and Papaw (um, who apparently did not get the message that I am not particularly enthused over the fact that someone made a doll of me, let alone the psychotic look in this doll's eye, or the fact that she is wearing overalls with a tiara and has this stupid banner that says SAVE THE WHALES on it)
- Both of the movies they have made of my life so far on DVD from Prince René (again, very funny. Not)

• A new tiara from Grandmère. Because you know no princess should be without a pair of tiaras, in case one tiara is no longer able to perform its duties, the backup tiara can be called upon to fill in.

So far, I've only gotten one thing I asked for—a PowerBook and an iPod from Mom and Dad, and a gift certificate to iTunes from Mr. G. At least now I won't be the only person in the entire tristate area who hasn't gone Mac yet. It doesn't look like I'm going to end up getting Military Xander or world peace or anything else on my list, but that's okay, I guess. I'm pretty much used to disappointment at this point in my life.

My present for Michael showed up by special delivery while we were at church. I had to pay as much for shipping as I did for the actual present to get it here on time, but I know it will be totally worth it when he opens it and freaks out over its incredible rarity and coolness.

Oh, it's Lilly's turn. She's opening my present

to her. I kind of wish now that I'd given her something else. I mean, since she doesn't seem to have any trouble finding romantic partners these days.

Oops. Lilly doesn't look very happy—

Yeah. The beach. That's how far I had to drag Lilly to keep the entire palace from hearing her screaming at me.

Why me? Really? Why do I even hang out with her? I mean, she's fun to be around when she isn't being like THIS.

But THIS is just ridiculous. She's STILL yelling about how I have no right to tell her that she is incapable of finding love when I know perfectly well that she and Boris Pelkowski went out for nearly a year.

Um, yeah, before she DUMPED him for another man.

Although I am not about to point this out to her. As if I could even get a word in edgewise.

But if I could, I'd remind her that it's not like I'm exactly thrilled with her gift to me, either. Contrary to what Lilly may think, I do NOT need to learn "how to express my ideas and stand up for myself" in my relationships, the way the title of the book she got me—*The Assertive Woman*—swears it will teach me. I am totally assertive. I pulled her out of the palace and made her come down here so she could go on screaming without disturbing anyone, didn't I?

Good thing I picked the beach, too. This place is deserted. Possibly because it's only, like, 50 degrees and totally cloudy out. Also because, um, it's Christmas. Everyone—except for us—is at home having a nice time with their family members probably doing that dumb olive-tree-branch thingie or at least watching *A Christmas Story*, but whatever. Even the cruise ship is getting ready to go. There's only one other boat—one of the ones that carries tourists from the cruise ship to shore—bobbing around out there in the bay, with just a few people in it.

Still, I bet they can hear Lilly's screaming, when the wind blows the right way.

"Why don't you just admit it?" she's shrieking. "You're jealous of the fact that while you have had only one boyfriend your entire life, in the past twenty-four hours, I've had THREE!"

"Three?" I seriously cannot believe this. "You're counting *Pierre*? Lilly, he's TWELVE."

"Thirteen!" Lilly looks furious. "And what's so wrong with a younger man adoring me? If it's good enough for Demi and Cameron, shouldn't it be good enough for me?"

"Lilly." Really, I don't know why I put up with her sometimes. "That's not the point."

"No, it isn't," Lilly yells. "Why don't we just admit the truth? You don't approve of my relationships with Lord Mulberry and Pierre because they're royals, and I'm not, and you don't approve of my relationship with Franco because he's a servant! You are such a PRINCESS!"

I am trying to be the voice of calm in the storm of passionate vitriol she is hurling at me, but it isn't easy when I feel so much like turning around and going back up to the palace. After all, that's where Michael is. Right now, instead of sitting on this knobby piece of driftwood writing this, I could be in Michael's arms. Well, if my dad wasn't looking, anyway.

"That isn't true, Lilly," I say, in what I hope is a

very assertive voice. "I don't approve of your relation-ship with Lord Mulberry because he is pro-hunting, as you well know. Besides, where can it go? As soon as he finds out the truth about your antimonarchist leanings, he's going to run from you like a startled fawn. And I don't approve of your relationship with Pierre because you're too old to be dating someone who is so short he can ride for free on the New York subway. And I don't approve of your relationship with Franco because it got in the way of his doing his job, and now, because of you, he has none."

"Like I held a gun to his head and MADE him punch Simon," Lilly says scathingly.

"You have a quality about you, Lilly, that some men—and boys—find hard to resist."

I don't WANT to say this, because it's kind of complimentary, and it isn't like I *want* to compliment Lilly right now. But it's true. It was the last thing the Comte de Brissac said to me as his parents were dragging him off to their Rolls. "Your friend has a quality about her," Pierre managed to choke out, as his father tried to stuff him into the backseat, "that no man could help but find intoxicating. Please tell her I will always love her, though others may try to keep us apart!"

"Uh," I'd replied. "Whatever you say, dude."

Still. There may be something to it. It would explain a lot about Lilly's—er—*varied* romantic life.

Lilly, much to my chagrin, looks flattered.

"Do I?" she coos.

I seriously want to throw up on her.

"Apparently," I say. "To tell you the truth, *I* don't see it. Lilly, don't you feel the least bit guilty over what you did to Franco?"

"You mean over what Franco did for love of me?" Lilly looks starry-eyed. "Don't worry about Franco, Mia. He'll be all right. He was only doing this footman gig until he can get the job he really wants, anyway."

"Which is?"

"Snowboard instructor in Zermatt."

"Well," I say. "Now he's going to have plenty of opportunity to work on that particular dream of his, isn't he?"

Is it my imagination, or are the people in that boat out there WAVING to us?

"Oh, that remark is just so like you." Lilly's stopped looking starry-eyed. She looks REALLY mad now. "Not the *real* you, of course. But the snotty you, the one you become when you're in Genovia."

"What?" Now I know Lilly's lost her mind. Clearly, she left it somewhere over the ocean during that transatlantic flight. "What are you *talking* about? I am *not* snotty."

"You so are." Lilly looks really peeved. "When you're in Genovia, you are. Admit it, Mia. You are totally two-faced. In New York, you act all shy and self-deprecating—you're the very definition of a teen suffering from chronic low self-esteem. But when you're in Genovia, it's like you're a different person! You have no problem telling people—in particular, your so-called best friend—how to act and what to wear—"

Okay, now she's gone too far.

"For your information, Lilly, I don't particularly

LIKE the fact that I have to tell you not to wear rude T-shirts in front of my grandmother, or that it's wrong of you to organize games of strip bowling during her party. You're the one with the two hundred and ten IQ. I would think you'd KNOW better. But apparently in cases like this, it's your EMOTIONAL IQ that counts, and we both know you aren't exactly *gifted* in that arena, now ARE YOU? So what choice do I have but to tell you what to do, since you apparently can't figure it out for yourself?"

Lilly flushes. But she isn't ready to give in.

"But back in New York," she shoots back, "you make fun of your grandmother for being so worried about clothes and parties. Back home, you're more concerned about global warming and overpopulation than you are about whether or not people show up at the breakfast table in their pajamas. Here, it's like you lose yourself in all this unimportant stuff, like tree lightings and Advent calendars—"

"That stuff isn't unimportant," I interrupt her. "Yeah, it's not as important as global warming, but it's *tradition*, Lilly. And tradition is important, too. So is respect. And it's disrespectful to come to breakfast in your pajamas when you're staying in someone's palace."

But Lilly still wasn't giving up.

"I'm not the only one you boss around over here," she declares. "You tell EVERYONE what to do. Franco and Antoine and that maid who brings you hot chocolate in the morning—"

"Because I'm their BOSS, Lilly," I explain. "What do you think being a princess *means*? I have to run an entire country someday. In order to do that, I'll have to give orders sometimes. It's not like I don't say please and thank you and try to be polite about it. But that's what princesses *do*. We *rule*."

For the first time, Lilly looks a little ashamed of herself.

"Well," she says. "It's just . . . well, I'm not used to it. It's weird to see you all . . . *ruling*."

"Michael doesn't seem to have a problem with it," I point out.

"Michael thinks it's hot," Lilly says, not without some disgust.

Whoa. Michael thinks it's hot when I boss people around? Maybe it's time I start bossing *him* around a little—

Oh, my God. That boat, the one with all the people on it . . . it's getting *really* close to the shore. And the people in it are totally shouting at us. I can't really tell what they're saying. But they look kind of upset. Some of them are scooping handfuls of water out of the boat and back into the ocean because—

BECAUSE THEIR BOAT IS SINKING!

Good thing the chefs counted on fifty for lunch.
There's plenty to go around.

Which is good, because the people from the
cruise ship are REALLY hungry.

The way they're going at the lobster bisque,
you'd think they hadn't had any food in weeks, when
in reality—according to Patty from Oklahoma—they
enjoyed a full breakfast buffet just a few hours ago.

But I guess being stranded can stimulate the
appetite.

Especially when, you know, you've paid 144 bucks
(54 for the under-twelve set, according to Patty, who
left her two kids back on board on account of the cost
and the fact that they just wanted to watch *Christmas
Country Bear Jamboree* on pay-per-view anyway) for
the privilege of strolling down the historic streets of
Genovia, enjoying its quaint shops and outdoor mar-
kets, only to find all the shops closed and the mar-
kets shut down due to it being Christmas.

And then, as if all that were not bad enough, to have your boat sink on its way back to the ship. As Daryl from Seattle keeps putting it, "Bummer, man."

This seems to pretty much sum up the feelings of Joan from New Paltz, New York. Not to mention Jessica and Mike from Goshen, Indiana, Ann and Rick from Ann Arbor, Michigan, and even Chris and Jake from San Francisco.

But things are definitely looking up—all the passengers keep assuring us—now that they've gotten to see some real live royals . . . not to mention eat with them and use some Royal Genovian Palace towels to dry themselves off.

I guess it would be putting it sort of mildly to say Grandmère was surprised when Lilly and I came back from the beach with the cruise ship people in tow. When we first walked into the Great Hall, where everyone was still unwrapping gifts, she took one look at the group behind us—shivering in their sweatpants and Tevas—and pressed her lips together so hard, they disappeared. Lilly later said she heard Grandmère mutter, "First cats. Now Americans.

What will she drag home next?"

But then her natural instincts as a hostess took over, and Grandmère sent Antoine off for towels, hot tea, and changes of clothes for our Christmas guests.

My dad wasn't nearly as sanguine about the whole thing. He immediately got on the phone and demanded to know why the cruise line hadn't come out to rescue their own passengers . . . not to mention where the Royal Genovian Coast Guard had been, leaving his daughter and her friend to clean up what should have been their mess (although, really, it hadn't been a biggie. We'd just yelled, "Stand up! Stand up!" when the cruise ship people's boat capsized and they were floundering around in the waves. They'd only been about five feet from shore. Even the toddler—Olivia, daughter of Janice and Paul from Reno, Nevada—had only been in water up to her waist).

But whatever. The Royal Genovian Coast Guard had totally been busy toasting one another with eggnog, watching the Yule log over their radar scanner, and listening to the Christmas carols over the shortwave radio, so they missed the boat (literally).

But, really, you can hardly blame them. I mean, it's not like boats sink in the Genovian Bay every day. This is our first one, that we know of.

Now Dad is trying to figure out what to do with them. The cruise ship people, I mean. He had the Royal Surgeon come over and check them out for hypothermia, considering the fact that they were soaked and all. But there's nothing wrong with them physically, except that nearly all of them have exceeded their body mass index, due to too many trips to the dessert buffet back on the *Princess of the Seas* (the name of their cruise ship).

And since they are very polite—much more polite, for instance, than a certain visitor from New York City—I mentioned that they'd be a lot less trouble-some houseguests than the royal ones who'd just left. My dad said he tended to agree . . . a statement that caused Grandmère's mouth to shrink even smaller.

But, being a princess, and all, she graciously offered Bud a seventh bowl of lobster bisque, which he just as graciously accepted.

I hope Lilly takes a good look at this and realizes

that there IS more to being a princess than just parties and clothes and bossing people around. There's also making people feel welcome and at home, and saving them from potentially drowning in two feet of water.

I hope she realizes that guests have an obligation, too, and that's to be polite and not get members of the household staff fired for hitting princes.

But this might be too much to hope for, even at Christmastime.

Patty says it's always been her dream to meet a real princess, so I posed for a picture with her and Bud, which Antoine said he'd be sure to mail to them, as soon as it's developed, since their own camera (fortunately, one of those disposable ones) got soaked down on the beach.

Then Patty announced that her other dream had always been to meet a queen. By that she meant Grandmère, and not Queen Elizabeth, who had left by royal helicopter last night just minutes after the fracas broke out. I tried explaining that Genovia is a principality, not a monarchy, and that Grandmère is dowager princess and not a queen. But Patty said she didn't care.

Instead, she got up from the table, marched down to where Grandmère was sitting staring in horrified fascination at Bud's mullet, and asked, "Your Majesty, can I have your autograph?"

I was worried for a second that Grandmère might say no. But at the last minute, she seemed to give up, and went, "Yes."

Then she scrawled her name in Patty's scrapbook—which, Patty told me, she takes everywhere, because you never know when you might run into a moment you need to record for posterity. She's already pressed a bud from one of the bougainvillea plants outside onto her new "Genovia" page, along with a tissue from the Kleenex box in the guest bathroom and a tuft of Rommel's fur that went floating by in the air.

I guess this caught Grandmère's eye, since she started flipping through the book, going, "And what is this?"

"Oh," Patty said, looking modest. "That's just my scrapbook."

"Your what?" Tante Jean Marie asked.

"My scrapbook," Patty said. And then, when she saw the three royal sisters looking blank, she laughed and said, "Don't y'all know what a scrapbook is? Why, I belong to three scrapbooking clubs—Rather B Scrappin', Scrap It, and Scrappy Scrappers. We get together two, three times a month—sometimes more— to scrapbook."

When Grandmère continued to look blank, Patty elaborated: "To press our precious memories into books so that we'll always have a timeline of events to show our children and grandchildren."

"Yeah, Grandmère," I said, embarrassed that my own grandmother did not know of this timeless American pastime. Even though, of course, my own mother is so violently anti-scrapbook that she took the one someone gave her when Rocky was born and hammered it shut with nails and barbed wire so now no one can open it. "How come you don't keep a scrapbook?"

Grandmère gave me the evil eye.

"Princesses," she said regally, "don't scrapbook."

"Well, that's a shame," Patty said. "It's very relaxing. And if you don't mind me saying so, Your Majesty, you look like you could use some relaxing."

Grandmère looked extremely offended at this. But Patty didn't notice. She flipped open her scrapbook and started showing Grandmère all the different places she and Bud and the kids had been on their cruise—Barcelona, Cannes, and Monte Carlo so far—chattering away about each of them.

Grandmère listened silently for a while, then, as Patty was waxing more and more eloquently on the fun she and Bud had had playing baccarat in Monte Carlo, she seemed unable to remain quiet a moment longer.

"I suppose," Grandmère said acidly, "that you'll go back to America and tell everyone that of all the places you stopped, Genovia was the worst."

But Patty looked shocked.

"No way, Your Majesty," she cried. "Why, I'm going to tell them Genovia was the best!"

Grandmère looked perplexed. "But . . . your motor launch back from Genovia to your ship SANK."

"Oh, that," Patty said, waving a dismissive hand. "Who cares about that? When I show everyone your autograph—you and your granddaughter's—they're going to be pea green with envy."

"Besides," Bud added, "you got way better grub here than they do in Monaco. Those mussels we had in Monte Carlo gave me the runs."

Hearing this, Grandmère blinked rapidly. I know it sounds unbelievable, but I could almost swear I saw a tear in her eye.

That's right. *Grandmère*'s eye.

I do know for sure that she reached out and squeezed Patty's hand.

"Thank you," she whispered. "You . . . you might be right. Perhaps I do need to take up this . . . scrap-booking."

Patty looked up from her "Christmas Trees Around the Mediterranean" page and said with a smile, "I think you'd be a natural at it, Your Majesty."

Which I'm pretty sure was the nicest thing any of Grandmère's guests had said to her all day. At least, judging by the way Grandmère smiled, anyway.

The cruise ship people got off safely. The *Princess of the Seas* sent another motor launch for them.

Our good-byes were almost tearful as we walked our guests out to the limos that stood in the palace driveway, waiting to take them down to the dock. Chris and Jake promised to write. Olivia fussed over the Madame Alexander doll of me that I'd given her. Patty promised she'd send us each a little mini-scrapbook of their two-hour stay in the palace, so long as Antoine followed through on his promise to send her the photos he'd taken.

Since that's Antoine's job, I assured Patty that he would.

So, after giving the cruise ship people a large hamper of food for their twenty-minute sea voyage—not to mention many of the other gifts we'd received and didn't want, such as the Dolce & Gabbana leg warmers Philomena got for me (good thing she is still in bed with that migraine), which Chris and Jake declared were totally fabulous, and Lilly's book on being assertive for Ann, and my book for her on finding the perfect man (we both agreed we don't actually need them anymore) for Joan—we walked them to the waiting limos, where Patty turned and said with tears in her eyes, "We just can't thank y'all enough for your generosity. If everyone in Europe is as nice as y'all, the rest of our trip is going to be super." Then, to Grandmère, she added, "I'll put your official Rather B Scrappin' membership kit, along with a 'Gettin' Started' handbook, in the mail just as soon as I get home, Your Majesty. You're just going to LOVE scrapbooking. I know it."

Then they all got into the limos, and the chauffeurs drove them away, toward the dock, and their waiting launch.

And I turned to Lilly and said, "SEE?"

And she said, "What?" all defensively.

And I said, "THAT is what it means to be a princess."

Lilly just sniffed and flounced back inside. As we followed her, Michael said softly to me, "Actually, I think that's what it means to be human, but no big deal."

Which of course he's right about. But I'm glad Lilly didn't overhear him, just the same.

And then we went inside to unwrap the remaining presents.

Still, I'm almost sure Lilly gets it now. She is being much more polite to everyone, and even let Rommel have some of her bûche de Noël.

Ooooh, there are only two presents left under the tree . . . one giant one (mine for Michael) and a medium-sized one (his for me). Grandmère just had Antoine hand them to us, and said in a tired voice (and who can blame her? After all, she's been through quite a lot in the past twenty-four hours), "Open them, please, so we can all go upstairs and nap until dinner."

But Michael, to my utter delight and astonishment, went, "Actually, Your Highness, would it be all right if Mia and I opened our presents for each other in private?"

And Grandmère looked relieved and said,

"Mazel tov," and headed straight for the Sidecar Antoine had waiting for her on a silver tray.

So I guess we are going to open our presents in private!!!!!!!!!

What could he have gotten me that he doesn't want everyone else to see????????????????????

Oh, my God! Michael is the best boyfriend EVER.
EVER.

We totally took our presents out to the garden,
where the royal gardeners finally got rid of the last
of the cats by putting bowls of vinegar around all of
the flower beds. (Cats don't like the smell and stay
away from areas the odor permeates. We discovered
this when Fat Louie was a kitten and decided to start
revenge peeing behind the futon every time I went to
Genovia. We kept bowls of vinegar there for a while,
and he totally stopped.)

So it kind of smelled less like bougainvillea out
there in the royal garden and more like salad dressing.

But that was okay. Because nothing could ruin
such a romantic moment. The sun even came out
from behind the clouds while we were there, making
rainbows in the jets from all the fountains, and down
in the village, the church bells started to ring for five
o'clock mass, and out in the harbor, the *Princess of*

the Seas tooted its farewell as it chugged off to Livorno, so it was way meaningful and all.

I told Michael to go first, so he pulled the wrapping paper off the poster I'd gotten him while I sat there on the edge of the fountain, anticipating his great delight over the extremely thoughtful and rare gift that I'd labored so hard to get for him and thinking about the huge French kiss it was likely to earn me.

But instead of delight suffusing his face when he saw Luke and Leia, confusion spread over it. Then he looked at me and went, "Where did you get this?"

I just laughed at my own ingenuity and said, "EBay! It's an original single-sided movie poster from 1977—"

"—in near mint condition," Michael finished for me. Somewhat to my surprise. Because how had he known what I was going to say? Unless . . .

"Michael." I felt a little sick to my stomach all of a sudden. And not because of all the bûche de Noël I'd ingested. "You don't . . . I mean, how could you already have one of these? I never saw it on your wall—"

"Because I won it off a *Star Wars* fan site last month," Michael said, starting to look amused about something. "I figured I could sell it and make enough to get you something you'd really like for Christmas."

I stared down at the poster, totally confused.

"But, Michael," I said. "This can't be the same poster. Because you were here when I won the auction. And if you were here . . . who sent it to me?"

"My dad. I asked him to take care of it."

"Your *dad*?" I couldn't believe it. "But . . . didn't he notice when the shipping address was the Genovian Palace?"

"Dad's not real detail-oriented," Michael said, laughing now. "I can't believe you were the one who bought my poster!"

I glared down at it. It didn't look nearly as nice as it had when I'd been wrapping it. Now it looked as if Princess Leia was kind of sneering at me. I couldn't believe it. First Dance Dance Revolution Party. Now this. Why could I never think of a decent gift to give my boyfriend?

"I'll sell it myself," I said, reaching out to grab the poster from him. "And buy you something really cool instead, something you'll really like."

"No way," Michael said, snatching the poster back. "This *is* really cool, and I *do* really like it."

"But." I felt terrible. "I got you something you already own!"

"Yeah," Michael said, still grinning. "And wanted to keep. And now I get to."

Then he set the poster aside and held out his gift for me. "Now you open yours."

Still feeling terrible, I undid the silver ribbon on the package he set in my lap. I am such a loser, I was thinking. Out of all the sellers on eBay, how had I managed to buy something for Michael *from* Michael? Why hadn't the Madame Alexander doll company made the doll of me waving a banner that says LOSER instead of SAVE THE WHALES? Because that would have been more appropriate.

Then I opened the box containing Michael's present to me, and gasped.

Because inside it was Military Xander, the one

Buffy the Vampire Slayer action figure I'd been missing.

"Oh, Michael," I cried, when I could finally speak. "It's just perfect!"

"Really?" He grinned. "I was hoping you'd like it. It's the only one you don't have, right?"

And then, as if someone had kicked me, I remembered.

I must have gone pale or something, since Michael's grin faded, and he looked at me with a suddenly worried expression.

"Mia?" he asked. "Are you all right?"

"Oh, Michael," I managed to choke out, feeling sicker to my stomach than ever.

I didn't want to tell him, of course.

But what if he came over and saw the gap on my windowsill where Giles had once stood?

"I don't have the complete collection anymore," I said miserably. "I . . . I sold Fiesta Giles so I'd be able to afford the poster for you."

The corners of Michael's lips twitched.

"You're kidding me, right?" he asked.

I shook my head. "I wish I were."

Michael made a noise. When I looked up, I saw—to my surprise—that he was laughing.

"Michael," I said bewilderedly. "Why are you laughing?"

"Why aren't you?" he wanted to know.

"Because this is your first Christmas in Genovia," I said. "And I wanted it to be really special. And, instead, everything's gone wrong! I thought at least I could get you a really great gift, but I couldn't even do *that* right."

"Well, I don't have a whole lot of experience with them—Christmas presents, I mean," Michael said, a little more seriously. "But I have to say, this one is pretty special. The best Christmas present I ever had, as a matter of fact."

"But how can it be?" I felt more and more miserable every time I looked at that stupid poster. "The best present you ever had, I mean? You obviously didn't want it in the first place if you *sold* it."

"Are you kidding?" Michael asked, pulling me into his arms. "The last thing I wanted to do was sell it. The only reason I did was to get enough money for something special for you."

"Well," I said, cupping a protective hand over Military Xander in case he was thinking of taking it away, like I'd tried to do with his poster. "The only reason I sold Fiesta Giles was to get something special for you."

"Well," Michael said, with another laugh. "Then we're even. And I love my poster even more now *because* you got it for me."

Really, what could I do after that, except kiss him?

It was a very long time after that that Michael raised his head and said, "Although the sight of your grandmother's face when she looked out into this garden and saw all of those cats? That was a pretty good present, too."

To which the only rational reply was, "Michael, shut up and kiss me some more."

And so he did.